Rotor

Lauren Leja

Nixes Mate Books
Allston, Massachusetts

Book design by d'Entremont
Cover photograph by Lauren Leja

"Rotor" originally appeared in *Midway Journal*

Of course, a gigantic thank you to Michael McInnis for making it all happen (again). With gratitude to Jack Gantos, Gary Lutz and Iris Smyles. And with endless appreciation for the perpetual support of Natalie Curley, Jim Linderman, Michael Martone and Anne Russo.

ISBN 978-1-949279-18-4

Nixes Mate Books
POBox 1179
Allston, MA 02134
nixesmate.pub/books

I Remember

I remember chalk.

I remember when green blackboards were new.

I remember a backdrop of a brick wall I painted for a play. I painted each red brick in by hand. Afterwards it occurred to me that I could have just painted the whole thing red and put in the white lines.
— Joe Brainard, *The Collected Writings of Joe Brainard*

Contents

Rotor

EGGS

Cheryl Putterham's magnificent ass was beloved by all the men of the High School, students and teachers alike. When Danny walked past the principal's office, he swore he heard Mr. Martin sigh and softly say, "My God, what a magnificent ass," as he watched Cheryl bend over to pick up her dropped pen. She tucked a snake of blonde hair behind her ear as she straightened up and smiled.

And of course Danny told everyone.

Cheryl was pretty but not beautiful in a movie star way. All her pluses and minuses kind of negated each other. Long blonde hair was offset by the crooked teeth (she refused to wear her retainer), her oddly graceful hands drew attention away from the scarred arms (crisscrossed with knife carvings and scratches) and that magnificent ass was neutralized by a flat as a pancake chest.

We weren't really friends but since we had to sit alphabetically, my M to her P, we were stuck together in Science and History. I was terrified of dissecting that stupid frog in Biology class and Cheryl was fearless, pinning its rubbery body to the tray and expertly slicing it down the belly. She folded back the skin, just like two doors, and pulled out all the organs, one at a time, and each was a different color.

Strangely triumphant, Cheryl held up every pink or blue or yellow blob with her long silvery tongs to compare it to the slides projected onto the wall screen. The smell from the formaldehyde made me dizzy and I spent the entire class in the nurse's office, sitting in front of the air conditioner and sipping warm ginger ale from a paper cup. Cheryl filled out our worksheets and forged my name on the top with hers. We got an A.

In Social Studies, I came to the rescue, letting Cheryl cheat off me during our daily quizzes of battles and presidents and proclamations. She never studied because she was always too busy with Steve the night before. Steve was her much older boyfriend and worked at the Muzique Centre at the next town over. It was spelled "Centre" because the hippie owner was a roadie for Led Zep a million years ago and spoke with a TV English accent.

Cheryl met Steve at the Centre while her boyfriend Tom was signing up for guitar lessons. She was wearing the world's smallest cutoff shorts and strategically bent herself over counters and stretched for things on the shop's highest shelves. A half an hour later, Cheryl was on the back of Steve's motorcycle, the tanned twin crescents of her ass stuck to the leather seat like suction cups. They rode to his apartment over his parent's garage and spent the weekend naked, listening to "Nights in White Satin" on repeat. And that was when Steve dared Cheryl to carve his name on her arm with scissors.

Cheryl was fearless but Steve always won.

During an endless filmstrip about the American Civil War, I saw Cheryl tenting her head with her unwashed hair and then suddenly run out the classroom door, her hands over her mouth. We all heard the retching in the hallway as she threw up in the water fountain.

Twenty minutes later, the school nurse came up to our classroom and silently collected Cheryl's bag and books. After class, I walked to Cheryl's locker to leave her a note, but when I got there, its yellow metal door was wide open. It was empty, except for some crumpled up quizzes and a single clog.

Cheryl was gone, erased.

• • •

Two weeks after Cheryl threw up in the hallway, the principal's voice honked over the intercom: "Will all juniors please report to the Cafetorium?" And the way he asked it wasn't really a question.

We grumbled down the corridors, snapping gum, pulling hair and giving wedgies. On the Cafetorium stage was a row of folding chairs, a giant cardboard box and a tiny table topped with stacks of egg cartons, a few floppy dolls, some lumpy white bags and a jar filled with folded papers.

Principal Martin took the stage. "Quiet down people and take your seats. We have a lot of ....um....information to get through this afternoon." And with that, the Home Ec teacher, the school nurse and the two gym teachers filed out onto the stage and stood nervously in front of the row of chairs.

Principal Martin cleared his throat. "We are here to address a very serious matter – teen pregnancy."

A few coughs in the audience and someone made a horrible puking sound and then everyone laughed.

"Parenthood is a very challenging decision that should never be taken lightly. Having a baby changes your life forever. Think about the proms you will miss or the college dreams that will" – Mr. Martin snapped his fingers – "Poof!! Disappear. Forever."

"First we will watch a film that may answer some questions you might have, and then, afterwards, we will all be engaged in an exercise."

The light flipped off in the Cafetorium and the film projector clicked on, throwing a white square of light against the giant curtains stretched across the stage. The image of each film frame rippled and undulated over the fabric and it was like trying to watch TV underwater. Cartoon sperm bombarded a lazy egg which quickly sprouted into a miniature baby. The narrator sounded like Mr. Magoo.

Then all pretense of scale and logic disappeared, and the tiny baby became an adult-sized baby with adult-sized teenage parents. The giant baby was crying in his high chair and then, most disturbingly, getting his diaper changed. It was like a very confusing Japanese monster movie with radioactive isotopes and without subtitles. Everybody spoke American.

I thought of the comic book sea monkey ads, with those giant shrimp doing all sorts of everyday human things. Somehow the ads made pearl necklace-wearing, briefcase-carrying, people-size brine shrimp seem completely and casually normal. And suddenly the crazy teen pregnancy movie with a six foot baby really didn't seem so unbelievable.

The film clicked off and we all sat shell shocked in the fake afternoon darkness.

"Imagine the size of the dump in that big baby's diaper," someone joked from the back row.

"Like the elephants in a parade with that poor guy following with the little shovel," someone else answered.

"Enough!" Principal Martin announced from the stage. Alphabetically, Principal Martin called each of us girls to the stage to draw an envelope from the big glass jar. "Ladies, open your envelopes. Inside you will find the name of your husband for the weekend. Each pair of you will become parents."

I ripped open my envelope. Tim R. R for reject. Retard. Ridiculous. Tim had big ears and chewed tobacco and swore a lot. I guess he was microscopically less embarrassing than being stuck with Chris who compulsively whistled and wore his clothes inside out, and John, the Chinese kid who already had a bald spot.

"Find your partner and pick up your baby from Nurse Smith," the principal instructed us. "And you will be graded on this."

I reluctantly shuffled over to Tim. His ears were so much bigger up close.

"Let's get this over with," he sighed.

"I know," I said. "It's just a weekend. How hard can it be?"

"It's gonna be the longest two days of my life," Tim predicted.

Side by side, we silently waited in line.

When it was our turn, Nurse Smith asked, "Egg or flour?"

"What? Where are the dolls, those Responsibility Babies?"

"Budget cuts. A few we had last year didn't make it. A lot of anger management issues. One was thrown off a bridge and another doll was somehow kidnapped from the food court at the North Shore Mall. You kids need to choose your baby from what's left – egg or flour?"

"Tim, what do you think? The egg is tiny but breakable. And the bag of flour is as heavy as a real baby but pretty indestructible."

"I think I don't care."

"Then I pick the egg," I told the nurse. I imagined a real baby with Tim's Dumbo ears and felt relieved that our kid was an egg.

"Most importantly," she said, "No hard boiling. And one more thing – family portrait time."

The Nurse pulled out a Polaroid camera and pushed Tim and me closer. "Hold your egg and say cheese."

The Nurse authoritatively pushpinned the photo onto the bulletin board. It looked like a half assed wanted poster. Tim is sneering, I'm panicked and the egg is a fucking egg.

"I'm headed to History," I told Tim.

"Bio is my last class," he answered.

"Who is babysitting the egg? And what should we name the baby?" I asked him.

"Fuck that – it's a fucking egg!" Tim answered and spit tobacco juice into his empty 7-up can.

"We need to work together to keep this egg alive until Monday or we will both fail," I begged.

Tim spit again. "Fuck that."

And then I realized I would both flunk and be divorced by Monday morning.

Very gently, I cradled the egg in my palm and carefully walked to history. In the classroom there were other babies, mostly bags of flour, and even one Responsibility Baby, flat on its back on the floor, like an albino turtle flipped over on its shell.

"No babies on the floor!" yelled Mrs. Williams.

Sandra groaned and grabbed her Responsibility Baby by the foot and pulled it onto her lap; the doughy fist dangled in mid air.

The lights dimmed. Mrs. Williams started up yet

another Civil War filmstrip. As troops blindly ran up hills at Antietam, I noticed my egg had moved, sliding down my imperceptibly crooked desk, a slow motion escape. A runaway egg was not going to make me fail this stupid experiment. I pulled off one sneaker and placed the egg safely inside it like a little playpen.

After class, I walked down the hall carrying my egg like it was nitroglycerin – slowly and protectively. Flying elbows, swinging locker doors, untied shoes – all suddenly became a silent menace. Was I experiencing an unexpected spasm of maternal instinct or simply the fear of flunking something so stupid?

I met up with Tim near the cheerleader's giant cardboard thermometer; they were magic markering the mercury to reach $300 for new pompoms.

"Your turn to babysit," I told Tim, shoving the egg into his sweaty hand. "Take it. I'm scared I'll kill it by accident."

"There must be something we can do to make this stupid weekend easier," he said.

"Come to my house," I begged him. "I think we can do pretty much anything we can to keep the egg alive until Monday. Maybe we can invent some sort of carrier?"

Miraculously that afternoon, the doorbell rang in a demented Morse code and Tim was standing on my front steps with his finger extended.

"I hope this is as painless as possible," he said, as he walked around the kitchen, foraging for food. Tim shoved a handful of giant pretzels in his mouth – it looked like he was chewing Lincoln Logs.

"I've been thinking," I told Tim, "about this TV show, a science fair. These kids invented all sorts of padding and parachutes so they could throw stuff off a roof. When the stuff hit the ground, they unwrapped it like tiny mummies. If it wasn't broken, they won a scholarship."

"What did they experiment on?" Tim asked, mid crunch.

"Lightbulbs, which seem like glass eggs to me. I think it will work for us."

Tim opened the fridge, took out the gallon of milk and chugged. All I could see was the bulging white square of the jug and Tim's big ears silhouetted against the bright interior of the refrigerator. When he finished, he had a ring of foam around his mouth like a rabid raccoon.

He burped. "Let's try to figure this science shit out," he said and wiped his mouth on his sleeve.

"There might be some stuff we can use in here," I said, as I started opening each drawer in the kitchen. I pulled out everything vaguely scientific – rubber bands, duct tape, a thermometer, scissors and string. Tim found the bread box and screamed triumphantly "Ta Da!" He held up a package of hot dog buns. "A perfect six pack of baby egg sleeping bags!"

"Exactly! Miniature sleeping bags is a good start but I think we still need some more egg protection. Let's poke around the house for anything else that might work."

I dragged out a saggy yellow plastic laundry basket. "Throw everything in here," I said. We split up and started ransacking the house for supplies. I poked around the places I normally avoided – under the kitchen sink, inside the bathroom vanity. I could hear Tim in other rooms; closets rummaged, drawers rifled, doors slammed. It was like being asleep while burglars were burgling a hallway away.

POP! POP! POP! Tim wandered into the kitchen.

The palest pink bubble slowly grew as he pumped his cartoon cheeks. It wobbled, herky jerky, from golf ball to grapefruit, then exploded.

"Shit!" Tim laughed and held out a fistful of silver foil wrappers. "I found a family pack of gum in the couch cushions and wanted to see if I could stuff the whole thing in my mouth. I can."

With two fingers he carefully peeled off the web of gum from his face, folded it, and shoved it back into his mouth.

"You ate all my gum?" I asked.

"I saved you one piece," said Tim and he pulled a stick from his back pocket, warm and bent in its yellow sleeve.

"This is disgusting but I don't care," I said, as I zigzagged it into my mouth. "It's like eating orphanage Juicy Fruit."

Tim pointed to a photo on the wall of a giraffe-like girl squinting at the sun. "This must be you – your legs still look like popsicle sticks"

I felt my face turn red. "What is important is that we become effective hunters and gatherers and get supplies for our egg."

We banged all through the house then emptied our armloads into the laundry basket. "It's like making a tiny Frankenstein monster with all this weird stuff." I said.

Tim laughed and presented me with a can of Cheez Whiz. "Very weird."

I extracted the silver tinfoil lollipop of a Jiffy pop. "Really?" The pile was like an autistic treasure hunt. Tube socks, a Halloween wig, a handful of band aids, a plastic L'eggs pantyhose egg, toothpaste, duct tape, balloons, a box of maxi pads and a toddler's life jacket.

"I guess this makes some sense." I carefully carried in our egg and tossed the package of hot dog buns on the pile.

"Let's build this contraption," I said.

We poked at the pile like mad scientists – pulling, wrapping, bending, rolling. Tim was embarrassingly motivated. "It's all about the layers," he said. "Like jawbreakers. Lots of layers to protect the mystery center."

I laughed. "Does that mean that you'll carry the egg in your mouth?"

"Blow me," answered Tim. "It's suddenly so clear how we will carry the damn egg."

Tim ripped the hot dog buns in half and tucked the egg inside. Then he cracked open the plastic L'eggs pantyhose egg, pulled out the suntan nylons and crammed the egg/bun inside. He squeezed in some Crest to fill in the empty spaces. "It's like spray foam", he explained, "but it tastes better."

I grabbed the toothpaste smeared egg. "Spearmint." I licked my fingers.

A lady in a nightgown was running across a pink box marked Extra Absorbent and I grabbed that too. I turned to Tim and explained, "These are NOT mine."

I pulled out a maxi pad and we both stared at it for a minute. "It's like a life raft," Tim said.

"For a squirrel," I answered.

"This will work," I said, peeling off the adhesive strips and sticking the pads all over the plastic egg.

Tim laughed. "I am not walking around with a Kotex football until Monday."

"Maybe I can disguise it."

"How? Draw a face on it?"

Tim pulled the cap off a red Sharpie and waved it

under my nose. I inhaled the oddly comforting magic marker scent. Somehow it's how I imagined the future will smell – vaguely antiseptic, dizzying, bright.

I drew a face onto the maxi pad-wrapped egg – cartoon lips, red scribbled hair, a colored in circle on each cheek. Slowly the absorbent cotton of the pads stretched the ink, fuzzy like tie dye, until the features doubled, tripled in size; the face now a distorted plastic surgery disaster.

"Close enough," I said. "Now we can celebrate. Open your mouth!" I commanded Tim.

I put my hand over his eyes and squirted a big orange coil of Cheez Whiz into his mouth. He coughed and swallowed.

"Me next," I said and shook the noisy can – click, click, click. The deliciously disgusting orange foam sputtered into my mouth until the can was empty.

We both laughed. Is this what married life was really like?

• • •

Saturday morning I opened one eye to an explosion of red hair on my pillow. A few seconds of sleepy soft focus and I realized it was the egg. But the egg wrapped in maxi pads and with a drawn on Pippi Longstocking wig. It was going to be a very long weekend until the Monday egg checkout at school.

I struggled down to the kitchen. My mother asked, "Where's the egg?"

"I left it in the bath tub."

"Young lady – you go get that egg or I will report you and you'll flunk! And flunking means summer school!"

In the middle of breakfast, Melanie called. "Party at my house tonight. My parents are going to a dental convention and put Sharon in charge." Sharon graduated the year before and was a shift supervisor at the Pizza Hut and everyone liked her because she gave out free breadsticks at the drive thru. "She is going to fake an appendicitis again and leave work early. Hopefully her car will already be filled with borrowed pizzas."

"I'll see you tonight. I have to bring my school baby."

Saturday afternoon I doused myself with Jean Nate, grabbed the blotchy egg and headed to Melanie's house. At the corner of Elm Street Tim whizzed past me on his bike, braked hard and looped back. As I walked, he rode around me in slow circles. I told him about the party and he invited himself. At the house, he hid his crappy bike in the bushes.

Tim and I could hear the thumping of music behind the front door and pushed it open. Two girls in denim cutoffs sloshed down the hallway with big red plastic cups and a shirtless guy carrying a bong wandered by, calling out "Cheryl? Cheryl?"

Tim grabbed a beer and put his palm on the floor. One of the stereo speakers was flipped face down and the floor was vibrating.

"Is this how deaf people hear music?" he yelled, as he pressed his face to the trembling floorboards. He put the egg on the floor next to the speaker. We watched the egg slowly roll another inch with each thump thump thump of the bass. Tim stretched out his hand like a starfish but the egg was too far away. I nudged it towards me with my sneaker and picked it up. "You are already a bad and drunk baby-sitter," I said. "You keep drinking and I'll take over."

Melanie's sister Sharon stopped me in the hallway. "Hey kiddo! Melanie is around here somewhere, the keg is on the patio and the pizza is everywhere. I'm trying to hunt down a lighter."

Buzzed and breathless, she grabbed my shoulder to steady herself.

"And don't forget – I have an appendicitis if anybody asks!" She wobbled off, patting down the pockets of her jeans for the millionth time.

The shirtless guy was pumping the keg and his friend in a leather vest, his thin blonde hair pulled back with a rubber band, was holding a 7-11 Slurpee cup under the spout. "Fucking foam!" he yelled at both the cup and his shirtless friend. They were the oldest people at the party.

"Let it rest a minute then try again," I said, surprising myself.

Vest Guy laughed. "You're a foam expert?"

"Actually yes. Sharon is a good teacher." Vest Guy was a familiar stranger. "Aren't you Will? I heard rumors that you broke a woman's fingers."

"I can neither confirm nor deny any alleged finger breaking," Will said. "But she deserved it." He winked.

"Oh." I shoved my fingers deep into my pocket. The egg shifted dangerously to the bend of my arm.

"Steve," grunted Vest Guy. Suddenly I realized that Steve was Cheryl's Steve, of Nights in White Satin fame.

"Is Cheryl here with you?" I asked.

"You know my old lady?"

I nodded.

"She's over there, under the trees." He pointed out into the yard, the cobweb tattoo on his hand stretching across his knuckles and the webbing of his thumb.

A fleshy blur beneath the backyard trees, the two bare legs extended from the shade. One foot had thrown off its Dr Scholl sandal and was almost glowing against the dark grass. I heard a rough laugh and then immediately a cough I would have recognized anywhere. I walked to the trees and Cheryl slowly solidified from the light and shadow.

Cheryl held out her left hand like the Pope. "Look." My eyes moved up from her chipped fingernails to the world's smallest engagement ring.

"Wow," I lied. "Congratulations!"

"Thanks," said Cheryl. She rested her palm on her belly, hard and round and bursting over her jean shorts. Cheryl sucked on her cigarette and exhaled a grey plume. Her giant hoop earrings tinkled like windchimes.

"What are you carrying?" she asked, waving her cigarette at my hand.

I had forgotten the egg.

"It's for school," I answered, totally mortified.

"Is that an egg baby under all those maxi pads? Jesus Christ. I know everyone is blaming me for them. Believe me, if I had a fucking time machine, things would be different."

I shook my head. "It could have been anybody." But me, I thought. "I was just freaked out when I saw your empty locker. It was like you never existed."

Cheryl's hand slid down into the sweaty plastic cup of beer wedged into the V of her lap. She sucked the foam from her finger. "Oh, I'm sure everybody is relieved to erase me. This baby is a pain in the ass but even hemorrhoids are better than high school," she croaked in the scratchy voice I remembered.

Cheryl noticed me staring at the purple bloom of bruises circling her wrist. "So who is your egg baby's father?" she asked, looking me in the eye.

"That guy Tim," I said, pointing. "The guy with the ears."

"I feel sorry for you. That kid will be jinxed."

"He's not so bad," I said unconvincingly. "I'm just trying to make it to Monday without the egg getting scrambled. This would be the most pathetic class to flunk."

Steve walked over coughing, and held out his pipe to Cheryl. He bent over to light it with a click click click of his lighter. I could hear her sucking on the pipe. She held the smoke, then suddenly pulled Steve's face to hers and exhaled into his mouth. Their heads crossed, the stringy blonde hair mingling, obscuring their faces. They melted together for that moment in the halo of smoke. It was weirdly intimate. Embarrassed, I looked away but Steve glanced up at me and grinned. He straightened up and rubbed his bare chest. The thick patch of hair snaking above his belt somehow horrified and titillated me. "You next?" he asked.

I ran away looking for Tim and found him perched on the picnic table, surrounded by crescents of pizza crusts. A few crushed beer cans dotted the grass, like toys squeezed by a strongman.

"Any pizza left?" I asked.

"Doubtful," Tim answered as he flipped the flap of the box next to him. "Pre-chewed okay?" he asked as he waved the last coagulated yellow and red triangle in the air.

"I'm desperate," I said, shoving the pointy end of the cold slice into my mouth.

Tim laughed. "I never knew how gross you could be. I kind of like it." He pulled me down next to him.

"Hey! Watch it – the egg!"

"The egg? I kind of forgot about it. I'm just like my dad. I'll see the egg on Christmas Eve if it's lucky."

"Really? I'm sorry. I didn't know." I said.

"It's actually kind of nice to be able to blame pretty much everything on him."

We sat there not saying anything. It was not quite dusk; the sun and moon were somehow both sharing the sky. An airplane passed overhead in slow motion; the thick contrails lazily dissolving into a lumpy vertebrae and then into tiny pieces that floated away.

Tim elbowed me. "We both need another beer. I'll be back."

I chewed on a pizza crust and looked at the egg. "You are a pain in the ass," I said to its magic marker face. I thought about Cheryl and her inevitable real life baby. I imagined a car seat on Steve's motorcycle, or maybe even a side car, and all three of them speeding down the highway on some great adventure. But then I also knew what would really happen – a flat tire, Cheryl breastfeeding the screaming baby in the Kmart parking lot, Steve rolling change to buy generic cigarettes. Even if I flunked the weekend with my egg baby, it would be better than being chained to a flesh and blood baby for the next 100 years. Anything would be. I stretched my legs in front of me like an L and then a V, and the egg escaped and rolled down the grooves of the picnic table and over the edge. It plopped onto the ground with a dull thud.

Tim ran over, beer sloshing out of the plastic cup.

"Are you the drunk Mom already?"

"Not yet," I laughed. "But I am headed in that direction." I slid the whole new beer into my empty cup. "Is the egg ok?" I asked Tim as he nudged it with his foot.

"Seems okay. No visible guts," he reported.

In the dull glow of light from the far off kitchen window, somebody found a partially deflated basketball in the bushes and threw it at the hoop nailed to the back of the garage. As the ball traveled through the air, a bright light flashed, like localized lightning, in the heavier darkness under the trees. The kid threw the ball again and the light flashed on, hesitated, then faded off. He stood there stupidly and then suddenly understood there was a motion-activated light triggered by the basketball. Then rapid fire, he threw the basketball up and down in front of the sensor. The light flickered on and off spastically, pixillating everyone in the backyard into a herky jerky film strip.

I squeezed my eyes tight. "I'm buzzed and I feel like I am having an epileptic seizure."

Tim laughed and drank his beer. "That's how I feel most of the time."

I suddenly realized I needed to pee. "Where's the bathroom?"

"Upstairs. The one next to the kitchen flooded an hour ago. Some jerk tried to flush their egg baby."

"Murderer!"

"Technically," Tim agreed.

"Wish me luck," I said, as I wandered into the house to find the bathroom. The basketball kept flying and the motion light kept flashing. I grabbed the egg like a blind person, one hand out, eyes closed, trying to find the back door in the sporadic darkness.

My hands touched leather and I realized I had crashed into Steve and his leather vest. Cheryl was sitting on a Styrofoam cooler wrapped in duct tape.

"Woah!" he said. "This party is like being at the fucking planetarium...but with beer."

"I'm just looking for the bathroom. Me and my egg." I held up the egg and shook it. Apparently I was drunker than I thought.

"Me too," said Cheryl. She stuck out her arm, horizontal, and Steve hoisted her up. She wobbled. "I think it's upstairs, near the garage," Cheryl said to me. "Maybe we can find some hidden parent pills in the medicine cabinet."

We wove our way to the kitchen door, the light still flashing in strange intervals. A few orange dots from the tips of lit cigarettes darted like fireflies in little clumps around the backyard.

As we stumbled to the house, the music got louder and the glow from the windows lit up the minefield of vodka bottles, abandoned Doritos, pizza boxes and crushed Coke cans. It was like crossing an invisible equator – everything turned Technicolor as we walked through the sliding glass doors; all the murky silhouettes from the backyard morphed into real, tangible, people. In the kitchen, Cheryl grabbed an orphaned beer off the counter. "Probably backwash," she laughed.

Johnny was leaning against the wall, talking and waving a Cheeto in the air as if he was conducting a symphony. He watched her drink. "No booze for pregnant ladies," he said.

"Fuck you," she said, smiled and bit into the Cheeto in his orange fingers.

Cheryl shrugged. "Everybody's a fucking doctor. Where's the bathroom?" He pointed to the staircase at the end of the hallway and shrank into the wall.

On unsteady feet, we made our way to the stairs. Kids were leaning against the walls and sitting on the floor, their legs haphazard, dangerous. A big puddle of spilled beer seemed to blossom as it soaked into the shaggy carpet.

Drunk teenagers were talking through the stair railings; their anonymous arms reaching between the slats, grabbing cups, lighters, passing asses.

I suddenly remembered those mornings driving with my mom to the supermarket, driving past the prison on the highway, and seeing those prisoner's arms sticking out through the window bars, trying to reach the sunlight. Blurry faces and those arms, those hands. That was the worst punishment I could imagine – fighting for even a fistful of the world.

I was leading Cheryl by the elbow like a blind person, and in my other hand, I was surprised to find I was still carrying the egg. The bathroom door was ajar and I pushed it open with my foot. Rachel was spitting blue into the sink. She took another swig from the mouthwash bottle, gargled and spit again. "Sorry. I just puked into the laundry hamper. My mouth tastes like shit."

Cheryl pulled down her jeans and sat on the toilet, letting loose a loud and relentless stream. Rachel carefully chose a toothbrush from the cup and poked it around her mouth then filled in her lips with a cherry Chapstick. "Minty fresh again."

I carefully rested the egg on the vanity and searched the drawers for a comb. Rachel looked at the egg and laughed. "You haven't killed that thing yet? I already ditched mine in the Kmart parking lot last night."

"No," I answered. "Not yet."

"Mothers of the Year," Cheryl cackled as she spun the toilet paper roll.

Rachel shrugged and squeezed past me and down the hall.

I studied my face in the mirror, parted my straight hair down the center with a yellow plastic comb, then tucked each half behind an ear. Cheryl flushed and looked at me as she zipped up her jeans. "Fix me up," she ordered and bent her head down. I traced a line down her skull with the tip of the comb and as the curtain of hair divided, she watched me in the mirror.

Cheryl handed me the nub of black eyeliner pencil from her back pocket. "My eyes too."

I outlined one eye in black with my unsteady hand, stepped back. "Total disaster. Your eye looks like a drunk coloring book." I licked my finger and tried to erase the black outline. Of course, it became worse.

Cheryl poked a white bundle on top of a pile of towels. There was a "My name is______" sticker stuck to it and KELLY was written in the blank space with a ballpoint pen. "A flour baby! Poor Kelly," Cheryl whispered to the bag of flour. "But at least you weren't left in the Kmart parking lot."

"Kelly and my egg can grow up together," I shouted.

"Don't forget the third baby," said Cheryl, rubbing her belly. "Baby Skynyrd. Lynyrd if it's a girl and Skynyrd for a boy. Steve guarantees it's a boy," she explained.

"Steve thinks of everything," I said.

"Sometimes," sighed Cheryl, as she rubbed her belly. "But not always."

Pop! Pop! Pop! Big bursts of noise and light filled the bathroom window from outside. We stuck our heads out and over the garage roof. The backyard was filled with hissing firecrackers and the dandelions of lit sparklers.

"A miniature 4TH of July!" I cried out.

"I wanna get closer," insisted Cheryl. "Let's go out

onto the roof." She karate chopped the screen like the Bionic Woman and it slid down the garage roof in a slow glide and disappeared into the darkness. "Help me out," she asked, as she struggled to crawl through the narrow window. Her belly was dragging.

"Isn't that dangerous?" I asked.

"It's safer when I'm drunk. I'm more flexible, I bounce back easier." Cheryl answered.

"Okay," I said as I pushed the hamper underneath her feet. She twisted and flipped and I shoved and she managed to corkscrew out.

"Now the babies!" she commanded. "This is a family field trip."

Shaking my head, I handed her the bag of flour and the egg out the window. Holding the flour baby with both hands, she nestled the egg on top and rested her chin on it. Carefully, like a tightrope walker, she glided up the gentle slope of the garage roof and then disappeared down the other side.

I pulled myself over and out. The night air was cool but the shingles radiated the stored heat of the day. The height terrified me.

Invisible, Cheryl called out, "Never look down, just ahead."

"I'm trying," I answered as I made tiny tripods with

my fingertips on the roof and slowly crabwalked over the peak. The grit of the shingles felt like it was erasing my fingerprints.

Cheryl was at the edge of the roof, reclining; her legs dangled over the gutter. Scuttling over, I carefully unfolded myself next to her. I relaxed into the roof and looked up at the dark flat sky. The bargain bin fireworks whizzed and wheezed in the air; bursts of glorious pin-wheels and ear shattering halos surrounded us. I was momentarily distracted from my terror.

It was hot and noisy and beautiful.

I felt Cheryl's hand touch mine and I spread out my fingers. Cold and sweaty and metallic, she slid a beer can into my palm. "I tucked it in my sock," she explained. Quietly we passed the beer back and forth. I noticed the bag of flour resting in her lap, the egg on top.

"There's one last science experiment we need to do," Cheryl said. We both sat up. Cheryl handed me the egg. I could hear the voices below us, the laughing, the pop popping of beer cans.

Cheryl looked at me.

"Which falls fastest? The egg or the flour?"

"Physics 101," I said.

We held our babies over the edge.

"1, 2, 3..."

ROTOR

We both knew it was the shittiest carnival in the Tri-State area but we were going anyway.

During lunch, Susan and I went out for a smoke break and just kept walking. We walked through the football field and into the skeleton of the bleachers. Underneath, in the grey coolness, Susan pulled out stolen Home Ec scissors and cut off her jeans into shorts. She stabbed the point under the faded ghost of her back pocket and started to circumnavigate each thigh, sawing the blue denim. The pale sliver of her skin slowly grew into a slice. One leg, two legs. Susan stepped out of the denim tubes like she was shedding an old useless skin, the fabric circles newly forgotten on the gravel, perpetually sticky from decades of spilled sodas.

My turn. I pulled my arms all the way inside my red Tshirt, my arms stiffened into a taut teepee, a cotton triangle. I held my breath as Susan started to snip with the stolen scissors, from my waist up to my chin. The cold tips of the scissors dotted my skin with a metallic rat-a-tat.

When she reached the neckband, my white skin burst out, like cutting into a giant baked potato. She knotted the ends under my bra line and smiled.

Susan shook a paper bag in my face. "We got this!" She unrolled it open – the bag was full of miniature bottles of booze. "I've been stealing them from my cousin the stewardess. Her apartment is like a bar for midgets."

"Renee?" I asked. Renee was leggy and had hair like a magazine. She always spoke very slowly and clearly, like she was reading cue cards.

"Yeah, Renee. There's some rum, some vodka. And a few with no labels that taste like nail polish remover."

Susan handed me two, then she tucked a few into her back pockets and slid the rest into her white knee socks. Her ankles were lumpy like shin guards.

Susan unscrewed a tiny bottle, drank half and offered me the rest. I pinched my nose and gulped it down. It was like drinking fire.

"Ready to roll," she said.

Newly ventilated, we walked a few blocks to the bus stop intending to ride to the end of the line. At midday the bus had only a handful of passengers – mostly sleepy-eyed old people and a red mouthed girl circling circling in a Word Find book. A man clutching a wrinkled plastic bag marked "_patient's belongings" stood up from his seat and of course sat next to me. I was determined to maintain an inch buffer zone between us, waist to knee, but I couldn't stop wondering what was in his bag. It seemed pointy and I swear it even moved.

At the last stop, only Susan and I and the Man with the Plastic Bag were left. Susan easily climbed off and watched me through the window. I waited for the Man to get off but he wasn't moving. I fake coughed. He was like a statue. Finally in an awkward synchronization, I flattened my palm over his plastic bag to feel the invisible contents like a half-assed Braille then scaled the next three bus seats and hopscotched to the door. On the sidewalk, Susan was laughing her hiccupy laugh.

"You're an idiot," she said, her eyes tiny as she struggled for breath. "And we're still not there yet."

Susan kept laughing/hiccuping at me as we headed out of town and toward the faint shapes of the carnival in the distance – the tiny triangles of tent tops, the faraway circle of the Ferris Wheel. A spindly tree like a lollipop met us along the road and we rested in the dark dust of its diagonal shadow.

"This sucks," I said. "It's taking too long and my feet hurt."

A tinny clatter and a noisy flash of yellow burst through the air and Susan jumped into the middle of the road, stuck a thumb in her mouth and then dramatically jerked it out with a hitchhiker's Fuck You.

Susan ran to the yellow as the yellow sped to Susan. You know when you are walking towards another moving object and for a brief moment it's hard to tell if that thing is moving towards you or away from you? It seems stuck in space, a two second illusion, until suddenly it is bigger or smaller than you thought; it appears or moves. Time snaps back.

The Lay's Potato Chip truck rolled to a stop at her feet and the driver swung out of the doorless door, gracefully carried by momentum and balancing on one foot.

"Ladies," he announced, "I'm here." His hair was wig-like and his blotchy face was an angry connect-the-dots.

Weighing the instant odds of two against one, we hopped into the potato chip truck.

"I'm Tom." His fingers were strangely long, stretched out almost like Silly Putty, with one hand on the wheel and one hand conflicted between the gear shift and the air.

Susan plopped on an upside down plastic milk crate up front and I sat on the weird hump between the seats that vibrated with each shift of the gears.

The hundreds of foil-y chip bags crunched at every bump in the road. The truck smelled like a magical cloud of potatoes.

"I never knew there were so many different sized bags of chips," I told Tom.

"Snack size, variety packs, standard, family size, industrial," he recited, that right hand counting out each word.

I settled back into the lifeboat-sized bag of crinkle cut chips and watched the landscape unspool through the hole where Tom's door should have been: Telephone poles, stop signs, billboards, a random car. Birds like parentheses coasted over the trees. It was the world's most boring movie.

We were starving and begged Tom for some food. He only let us eat the failed experimental flavors, the discounted disasters, like tartar sauce and dill pickle, that even the prisons wouldn't order, and we munched and watched the far off shapes of the carnival become bigger and real.

Susan pulled a nip bottle from her sock and passed it to Tom. His long fingers held it carefully like a science experiment. "Don't worry, I'm not trying to poison you and steal your truck," laughed Susan. "Besides, I can't drive a stick."

Tom drank. Tom's relentless voice was a blurred abstraction, like the teachers in Charlie Brown. Susan methodically tossed every other potato chip out the truck window, a Hansel and Gretel trail of evidence, just in case.

Ten minutes later I watched Tom watch Susan suck the salt off her fingers, one by one. It was time to go.

We asked Tom to drop us off at the next pay phone near the bridge so we could pretend to call our Moms. I grabbed two bags of ketchup-flavored chips and Susan and I held them up to our foreheads, like puffy sun visors, as we loitered at the pay phone until Tom drove away. Flip flapping the metal hinged return flap, I found a wedged disc of petrified gum sandwiched between two pennies. I tried to flip it – heads or tails – but realized both sides were the same.

When we walked the three more half moons of the bridge, we knew we were close to the carnival. Susan threw her bag of chips into the air like Mary Tyler Moore's hat and caught it with a defiant two-fisted clap. It burst with a pop and an explosion of potato chip confetti over our heads.

Susan sprinted ahead of me and found the jagged sections of the not-quite-assembled carnival fence. We walked through a limp gate and into the carnival grounds. The sun was too bright and we were too early;

workers were still setting up the midway. The food trucks clustered at one end, their windows and doors opened wide. The smaller games were in trailers, with sides flipped open like aluminum wings, and the bigger games were plopped in the center under plywood and canvas roofs, strung with Christmas lights. The rest of the field was filled with the noisy beginnings of the mechanical rides – hammers and shouts, thuds and clanks. Snakes of electrical cords, yellow, red and blue, S'd out across the patchy grass. The air smelled like high school – sweat, weed and french fries.

Susan and I wandered around, trying not to trip, looking fake busy so we wouldn't get kicked out. Everyone had a job to do, even the little kid carrying a cardboard box full of light bulbs. The men had the nonchalant fluidity of the well-practiced, smoking without hands while pounding in tent stakes or dragging sheets of plywood with thin ropes. An oval-faced woman with a cigarette laugh jabbed inside a gigantic ice machine with her scoop and yelled "You fucker!" into its noisy cavity. Dogs chased each other through the aisles of trailers. Even their barks seemed tired.

I ripped open my bag of chips and offered one to a dog. He barked a feeble bark and extended his face towards my fingers. His teeth were small and sharp. We ate the whole bag.

I looked around at the slowly assembled carnival, the gradual crescendo of noise. I didn't want to see the carnival stretch and grow and come alive, powered by all those hands and grunts and pulleys. I needed to walk into a readymade dream and get swallowed into a Technicolor world of junk food and roller coasters and spin art. The relentless sunlight had bleached the magic from everything.

This was the world of the mundane, the chipped and the broken. I didn't want to see how things really worked, the daily grind of the worn out and the disappointed, the mechanisms. I wanted to see the fake world, the world that would appear at dusk, under the promise and disguise of darkness. I realized I didn't want to share my chips with the sad dog – I wanted to walk a ridiculous invisible dog on a starched, rhinestone leash. I imagined myself with the empty leash, bobbing side to side, like a needle searching a compass, walking a dog nobody, including myself, could see.

A guy who looked like Jesus and wearing denim cut offs staggered by, lugging huge plastic bags stuffed with plush animals, over his shoulder, Santa-style. When he got to the Whack-a-Mole trailer, he pitched the bags over the counter and shouted "Ger-On-I-Mo!"

Susan turned to me and we both laughed.

We wandered, trying to waste the daylight. The crooked rows of the carnival were like the misshapen grid of a small city, arms radiating out from the biggest tent and the Ferris Wheel.

Almost imperceptibly, the dimmer switch of the sun was being turned off. Slowly the crisp edges of things got fuzzy, dissolved. The creeping twilight softened the world before the carnival lights switched on. Sounds somehow became brighter and sharper.

We took a left at the Tilt-A-Whirl and meandered down an aisle of campers, pup tents, and vans. Makeshift clothes lines stretched from the side view mirrors to trees and some upside down shirts hung, flapped low to the dusty ground. Inside out jeans were spread out on the tops of a few tents, their wet weight sagging down the roofs like pairs of legs. The sole of a foot poked out from the slit of one tent. A van was parked sideways, doors slid open; a partially deflated bright blue air mattress dripped over the edge. The van smelled like wet newspapers and instant coffee.

The redhaired girl was thin lipped and wide hipped. She slowly walked past us, hips like a metronome, with a tin of sardines in her hand. I had never seen anyone eat sardines, just old people on TV who didn't want to eat cat food. The red haired girl plucked out a tiny fish and held it over her mouth, an expectant seal. She bit off half, the salty tail still pinched between her fingers. I could smell the ocean.

"I'm starving," I said to Susan. I walked over to a food truck and looked inside a glass case at the giant baked potatoes wrapped in tin foil, split and bursting. "They look like shiny pillows covered with butter."

"If I wanted something healthy I would have stayed home," Susan said. "I want something terrible and delicious, like a deep fried Snickers bar. But I'd settle for a pickle on a stick," she laughed.

A little boy sitting on a yellow plastic milk crate looked up – his lips were stained an unnatural purple, like frostbite or some forgotten disease. He crushed the waxy paper cone in his chubby fist as he crunched the fluorescent shaved ice. He saw us watching him and stuck out his blueberry tongue. "That's exactly what my kid will do," Susan laughed as she gave him the finger.

Above us, around us, the sky was greying. Sparse lights dotted the Midway. The Corn Dog trailer was yellow and glowing like a topaz. Cartoon corn dogs danced along the cut out windows; one wore a top hat.

Susan tap tap tapped a nip bottle of vodka on the counter. "Trade?"

The lady at the corn dog concession looked around

and nodded. Her eyebrows were like boomerangs hovering over her small eyes. Her magic markered nametag said Beverly. She pushed open the trailer door with her hip and leaned back on the silver door after it slapped shut.

She was a bisected Beverly – the top half all ropey in a nicotined Tshirt and the bottom half, solid and bulky, her legs like furniture. A brassy Harley Davidson belt was her leather equator.

"Shit," Beverly said, flick flicking her plastic lighter. "You girls got an extra smoke too?"

Susan said, "Yeah, we'll trade you for two more."

Beverly went back in and grabbed two deformed corn dogs out of the tiny food tanning booth. Susan jammed it into her mouth like a doughy lollipop. The bright red dot of the cigarette lit up the center of Beverly's face in a soft orange circle. For a minute we were all three of us quiet and happy. I fanned my mouth with each bite, exhaling steam and pretending I was in Antarctica. Susan was chewing and waving her corn dog in the air as she babbled at Beverly. We drank giant Cokes from sweating cups the size of trash cans. Then when they were half full, we emptied some rum into them, stirring the drinks with our pointer fingers.

We stopped by the spin art booth to watch a girl with a yellow braid, thick like an animal's tail. She bobbed her head and circled her hand over the spinning paper discs, trying to understand the rhythms of the machine, the mechanics of the color. Finally nodding yes, she picked up a plastic bottle of paint in each hand and squeezed, systematically, and then punctuated with a squirt.

Susan peeked over her shoulder – "It looks like a bunch of butterflies in a blender!" She laughed. "And I'm already bored! Let's go win something."

"Pop my balloons!" the girl with the midriff yelled at passersby, mostly men. Her hair was crimped brown with blonde stripes, like burnt bacon. She wore jeans unbuttoned and flapped open; her deflated belly filled the acid washed V. Hanging below was a bulging canvas money pouch, filled with quarters.

"I want to win a bunny-on-a-stick!" decided Susan and she slapped down coins on the counter. The girl with the bacon hair was surprisingly graceful as she disappeared the quarters and, pivoting, offered Susan a fistful of darts.

On the wall was a big grid of quivering balloons, white and firm and slick. Low in the bottom corner two shriveled balloons dangled from their blue thumbtacks, as if someone had run out of breath before reaching the end.

"Even a moron can win," Susan laughed and the girl rolled her eyes up towards the crispy bangs.

"Knock yourself out," said the girl as Susan threw her

first darts wildly – gutterballs all.

I guided her hand. "Here, hold it like a pencil." We threw in pantomime – like launching a paper airplane over and over again.

Susan pushed my hand away and threw. Pop! Pop! Bounce. Pop! Bounce.

Susan clapped.

The girl smirked. "Even a moron can win. Pick your prize – pink or blue?"

Susan picked a pink bunny dangling from a bamboo stick and twirled it like a majorette.

"Perfect."

Now I was determined to win a prize. I wandered the Midway, sucking on the surviving ice cubes from my giant Coke and spitting them back into the empty paper cup.

The kid had a smashed nose and a reluctant shirt – one sleeve chewed away and every button somehow missing. He was surrounded by rows of shimmering plastic bags, each knotted and filled with a single lethargic goldfish. I had found my game.

The sign read, WINNERS ONLY. He said, "Everyone a winner!"

I asked, "Even me?"

He laughed. "Probably."

There was a wooden platform cluttered with glass fishbowls of all different sizes. Some were smaller and painted gold. Those were the ones that won you a goldfish in a plastic bag.

Throwing a ping pong ball is like throwing air – weightless and directionless. It was impossible to give a ball any force or guidance – it cluttered and sputtered and ricocheted. The kid with the smashed nose was Paul and he seemed to take my failure personally; he handed me a second, then a third, free bucket of pingpong balls.

I threw and threw. Paul sighed then looked left then right then behind us, before he slamdunked some runaway balls into the golden fishbowls. "We have a winner!"

"Oh!" I said, then silently mouthed thank you.

Paul handed me a plastic bag filled with water; the fish inside swam in sad circles. He shook his head. "Everyone a winner!"

I held my plastic bag fish up to my face and kissed him, my lips puckered just like his. "You look like a Freddie to me."

Behind us someone was having an explosive coughing fit. I turned around to see a guy with a plastic axe sticking out of his head, smoking a bent cigarette and choking. "Shit!" he croaked.

"Can I touch it?" I asked.

"Touch what?" He laughed.

"The axe."

He puffed on the cigarette. "Be my guest."

I reached out and jiggled the axe handle. It was attached to a cheap wig that shifted on his head. Blood oozed in the matted hair. "Taste it."

I dipped my finger in. It was sweet.

"Strawberry jam. It slides off my head but it looks so much creepier than ketchup."

Someone screamed. "Corey!"

"Shit – that's me. I gotta go back to work." He blew a misshapen smoke ring that stretched and drifted and lazily dissolved. "Come see me in the Mansion of Death," he called over his shoulder as he hurried away.

Plopped in the center of the Midway was the control center, the heart, of the carnival – the ticket booth. I expected to find a very important person inside, someone serious, vaguely authoritative, like the Wizard of Oz pulling all the strings. Instead, there was a teenage girl; she had explosions of freckles on her face, arms and throat. I handed her my folded five dollar bill and she handed me an accordion of ride tickets. She was reading a horoscope magazine, underlining parts with a red ballpoint pen. "Here," she said. She was the kind of girl that talked with her eyes closed.

I shoved the tickets into the waistband of my shorts.

Susan rescued another bottle from her socks. We filled our mouths with the orphaned ice from our Cokes and poured in a tiny vodka. I gargled and the ice cubes clanked against my teeth.

We wandered the Midway and stopped in front of a giant, shiny igloo – The World of Mirrors. The building was two stories tall and covered in a mosaic of mirrors; a crazy glittery slide that seemed stolen from a Las Vegas swimming pool ran from the roof to the dirty ground.

"We gotta go in!" squealed Susan. The bored kid wordlessly took our tickets and we clumped up the metal steps into the disorienting world. The first room was lined with mirrors – wavy metal reflective ribbons. Susan magically pulled out another pair of nips. We clinked the miniature plastic bottles together in a noiseless toast, guzzled them, and dramatically tossed them over our shoulders.

Standing in front of each fun house mirror, I saw myself contorted, pulled and pushed. Susan and I did a tug of war at each mirror, making instant before and afters. I became the fat lady with a tiny head. I flapped my arms that transformed into tentacles. I shrunk down into a stubby human ice cube.

We gyrated, watching ourselves become grotesque in seconds, manipulated like a comic strip transferred onto a chunk of Silly Putty and stretched. And then a step to the right, a smooth flat panel, and we were ourselves again.

We spun through a revolving door that opened into a teeny room, the size of a phone booth, lined with mirrors. Even the ceiling and the floor. It was claustrophobic, dizzying, coffinlike. I put out my hands to steady myself, closed my eyes and rested my forehead on the cold glass. It was like ice. Susan grabbed my elbow and wheezed into my hair, "I feel like I'm dying." I felt her words on my neck but saw her face and mine all around us, faceted and everywhere. It was weird to watch yourself, to surround yourself, an out of body experience that felt almost televised. My fingers traced the edge of the wall and walked themselves down the slimmest of passageways then pulled me after them. And I pulled Susan.

The tunnel opened onto a big space paneled with dozens of mirrors of all different sizes. We saw hundreds, thousands, of ourselves reflected back. On a jagged wall, I saw endless accordions of me, stretched to infinity. The room was a reflective igloo.

"I'm too confused and buzzed to figure this out" Susan whimpered.

I looked up at the ceiling and my lost face looked down at me. All around were our endless selves, both life size and microscopic, reflected in the complicated mosaic of mirrors, watching us and being us. The boundaries blurring, skin and glass; the soft pulsating world morphing into an angular silver universe. The discoballness of the walls flashed metallic and still animated with streaks of fleshy peach as we shifted, breaking down our movements into Star Trek cubism.

Then Susan pulled me down to the floor next to her. "I need to be rescued and I don't care how," she cried out in a voice part laughing, part panic, part drunk. "S-O-S!"

I could almost see her shouts bouncing off the walls, ricocheting between the dozens of our faces. I rested my cheek on her shoulder and waited.

"I don't want to die in here, looking at my own dumb face," Susan wailed.

"I think we can last 72 hours without water," I told her and laughed and closed my eyes. I heard faint sounds that became closer and louder, and separate and identifiable – giggles and bubblegum bubbles bursting. A little girl's head poked itself into our cell. "You okay?" she asked, punctuating it with a pop.

We were being saved by an 8 year old girl with gum in her hair and a faded Hawaiian Punch Tshirt.

"Thank god!" cried Susan.

The girl giggled. "My brother sent me in when you didn't come out. It happens all the time but usually it's the confused grandmothers. You can follow me out, but just so you'll know, use your hands, and just take every right turn – right, right, right, right."

Susan and I x'd our arms and 1, 2, 3 we hoisted each other up. We followed the girl, just like she said, four rights, and the rope of her braid flopped side to side.

We were dusty and drunk. I was shocked to find Freddie in his plastic bag, still crumpled in my fist. We both survived the House of Mirrors and I had somehow managed to not kill him.

The three of us sat on the dirt for a few minutes, recovering. My knees and palms were coated in a fine film of earth.

A guy in a red Tshirt and gold scarf walked towards me and I realized he was talking to his scarf and his a scarf was a snake. I stopped right in front of him and asked him directions to the Rotor. He had hands so dirty they were shiny and he pointed into the distance, making shapes in the air. My hand had a life of its own and my fingers traced the pattern on the snake's skin. He was tense and heavy and thick, a shimmery coil of muscle.

"I bet you already forgot the directions," he laughed, and he crossed his palm protectively across the snake.

I attempted to recreate the Snake Man's instructions, following my own finger in the air. I cut behind the Zipper, then The Tilt-A-Whirl, past the wall of screams from the Sizzler. I got tangled in the lacy 8 of forgotten panties, rolled down from the waist to ankle and left in the patchy grass.

Susan and I were feeding each other french fries with those tiny wooden pitchforks and laughing when an enormous guy with Stretch Armstrong arms casually approached us. He shook out a large paper coil of ride tickets in front of our faces.

"Ladies, I have a proposition for you." His tiny head and giant cartoon body distracted me from his actual words. His voice was kind of Southern and all the syllables were dragged out, doubled, tripled, like a sports announcer. LLLaaddeezzzzz.

Susan's very loud YES snapped me out of it. "What did you just agree for us to do?" I asked, assuming we were a package deal.

"We're going to help out John. We're going to work in the dunking booth..."

"...as dunkees." I finished her sentence. "But you can't swim."

"I won't need to," answered Susan. "John promised me nobody ever hits the target hard enough."

I hoped Susan knew how to float.

We followed John past the skee ball and the dime

pitch games and up to the big Plexiglas box with a ladder bungie-corded to one side. A garden hose ran up the outside and down the inside, the water gushing to fill the big box. The flow was randomly interrupted when a van drove over the hose, one axle at a time.

"It's easy," said John. "All you have to do is sit there and smile."

He took Susan's hand and helped her up the ladder like she was Miss America. Susan climbed down into the tank and shimmied out onto the hinged seat. Her red sneakers dangled a few inches over the top of the water.

She patted the place next to her. "Karen!" she shouted through the dunking booth.

I held Freddie up to my mouth and kissed him through the plastic and carefully plopped the bag onto the grass. It collapsed and spread wide; his crystal clear and shapeless universe suddenly had a bottom, a green green base. Freddie darted pointlessly at the ground, trying to taste the grass through the invisible barrier of the plastic bag. I untied my sneakers, lined them up next to Freddie and climbed into the tank. The hinged seat swayed and strained as I awkwardly crouched next to Susan, then unfolded my legs one at a time. My big toe skimmed the water.

Susan excitedly grabbed my hand and we both looked

through the streaked plexiglass cube at the crowd watching us. Our breath fogged the transparent walls and their faces were blurry and vague. Droplets of water raced down in rows like a beaded curtain. There was a new soft glow of the sunset and the systematic click click clicking of the carnival lights switching on, section by section.

A teenage boy who was all forehead and acne handed John his ticket and John piled a pyramid of softballs at the kid's feet. The teenager rubbed a ball on his pants leg as if he was polishing an apple. And then he threw it. Susan whistled and waved at him and I punched her in the arm – "Shhh!" The ball missed the target on the side of the booth by a foot. Susan laughed and pulled her shirt over her head. Now I had to laugh. The kid with the terrible face missed again and again. Susan stuck her tongue out and he gave her the finger as he shuffled away.

Next up was a little girl on her father's shoulders. Through the foggy walls of our tank she looked like a monster, all heads and arms and legs. Each hand handed John a ticket and he counted out twenty balls from the suddenly bulbous hammock of his Tshirt; the weight pulled his vneck down, taut, to his belly button. John stood in front of the father and daughter, she shrieked "Go!" and all four arms grabbed the balls and threw wildly at the target. Most crisscrossed and hit each other, negating the effort; the little girl tossing hers like a too-warm can of soda out the car window. The intensity scared us. "We're goners," I told Susan and took her hand, ready for our carnival baptism. I watched the flurry of arms and circles through the steamy hazy tank and heard the heavy thuds banging the walls. I closed my eyes and squeezed Susan's fingers tight. There was silence then suddenly, fists and feet, punching and kicking, shook the walls, making the water vibrate and bounce in concentric circles, like shock waves emanating from the epicenter of an earthquake. The suddenly furious little girl and her father wanted to kill us.

I braced myself flat handed against the wall before I realized we were safe – the dunking booth was a fortress. John, his overstretched shirt now drooping like a deflated Santa suit, grabbed the man's arm – "Don't fuck with my tank!" The man knelt down and the girl crablegged off his shoulders, magically returning into mere mortals in search of a Slurpee.

We were still dry and Susan was feeling invincible. "Just one more," she pleaded. "John promised we were done after three throwers."

"I miss Freddie," I complained, thinking of him swimming in his collapsed plastic bag purgatory. "This is the last time."

The daylight had faded and different lights came sputtering on in a drunken procession. Chunky Christmas lights strung from wires, tent to tent, made pinpricks of brightness in the new almost darkness. Long tubes of light came down from the giant bulbs at the tops of heavy poles that lined the perimeter of the carnival.

Slowly the rows squeezed itself open and a motorized wheelchair buzzed up to the dunking booth. A woman in a faded pink track suit, her very thin hair pulled tightly back with a rubber band, clutched the joystick with a claw-like hand. "My turn," she croaked.

John took the zigzag of tickets from her hollow lap and replaced it with a pile of balls. I couldn't understand how she was going to throw anything with her frozen lobster hand.

Susan cackled – "This will be quick!" She crunched her own hands into angry C's and pantomimed throwing knuckleballs inside our cube. I punched her for her rottenness and for doing it in the Lobster Lady's face and with so many people watching. Nobody deserved hands like that.

John rummaged behind the dunking booth and connected the duct-taped extension cord to a car battery on the ground. A windmill of colored discs started spinning, throwing rainbows into the box from behind. Bubbles and jelly beans of red, yellow and blue floated and melted all around us, like a silent discotheque.

The mechanical sun behind the tank reduced us to shadows inside it. Susan and I sat on that shelf, between the air and the water, and it was as if we were suspended between outer space and the sea, in the limbo of this world , and we held hands and waited for the fluke knuckleball to hit its target.

As the Lobster Lady spastically threw her last ball, the boy with the Terrible Face ran out of the shadows. With a triumphant smile of sweet revenge he punched the dunking booth target with both hands, then looked into the tank at us and mouthed "Fuck You."

The thwack of the target jolted the cube and the bench collapsed, dumping us.

The water was shockingly cold. The semi-darkness and haze of the tank was a mysterious and strange ocean. For a few seconds we were a confusion of arms and legs and mermaid hair, struggling to get our bearings in a slow motion underwater ballet.

When we stopped fighting we floated to the top. The tank was smaller than it seemed and we stood up, our chins over the waterline.

Deflated, defeated, we climbed out of the tank, grabbed our sneakers and Freddie and left the scene of our humiliation. Our wet clothes were fused to our bodies making our limbs stiff and robotic. Herky jerky, we walked down the Midway, hair stuck to our faces like seaweed. We were idiots.

A smirking kid at the Pickle on a Stick handed me a roll of Bounty and I wrapped my dripping hair in a paper towel turban. Susan bent at the waist and I wound the roll around her head until it became a white volcano, her ponytail erupting from the peak. Then I tucked one end of the paper towels into the neck of her Tshirt, like a bib, and said, "Hands up and spin!" She spun. Then I self-upholstered myself, from neck to knee.

We walked the Midway, puffy and damp. Civilians assumed we were some sort of bargain basement carnival act and the carnies just shook their heads. We looked like cartoon avalanche victims. My soggy sneakers squished noisily as we wandered around. I could feel the paper towel layers hijacking the wetness into itself.

The kid who was running the Rotor was leaning back onto the red metal silo of the ride, one foot flat, the other knee bent like a human number 4. His giant knuckles casually rested on the control joystick marked ON/TILT/ SPIN/OFF. Susan walked over to him and I watched them talk. Susan pumped her flat hand up and down next to her head as if she was measuring the uncertain heights of an imaginary family. He laughed, she laughed. He alternated his bent legs – 4, 4.

"Here!" She said and pointed at me. I shuffled over. "You can't ride the ride like that," he said. "Hold steady." He pulled out his pocket knife and slid it under the bottom edge of Susan's paper towel cocoon and gently sliced upwards. It crumbled open like wet bread.

Susan tugged at her Tshirt, reinflating it. When he turned to me with his knife, I flinched. "You're next," he said impatiently, as he sawed through my layers.

With his right hand, he hoisted Susan into the Rotor and with his left hand he slapped her ass square on the pocket. The door was rounded like a submarine and had a little window at eye level. I kicked the blobs of wet paper towels off the platform and the kid helped me in too. I waited that embarrassing millisecond for the thwack that never came.

Susan asked, "Maybe the centri-fungal force will dry us out?"

"Fungal? No, FU-gal," I laughed. "It will dry us out while it makes us stick to the walls."

The door slammed and clicked. The Rotor was a giant tin can with the lid sliced off. Skinny stripes of neon wrapped the top edge like a brilliant crown. The walls were black and painted with cartoony planets and stars, like a science fair planetarium. A voice shouted out of the tiny, tinny speaker mounted above my head: "Everyone stand against the walls, backs straight, both feet on the floor, hands by your sides. If you wear glasses, please remove them and put them someplace safe."

We watched the others adjusting themselves. A brother and sister who must have cheated to pass the height requirement started to giggle and I realized they were twins – red hair and braces and matching striped shirts. A brave (or oblivious) grandma tucked a tissue underneath her watchband while next to her a short, middle aged man in a suit, like a ventriloquist dummy, nervously whistled. Double dating teenagers mercilessly tickled each other. One girl snapped her gum and blew the biggest bubble I had ever seen. It grew in puffs and hovered in front of her face. Her date popped it with a stab of his pointer finger; a cloud of gum covered her eye and blunt bangs like a pink blindfold.

The metal walls and floor had soaked up the heat from the morning sun and were warm to the touch, feeling almost alive. I lifted my foot and watched the wet footprint slowly evaporate on the floor as if I was never really there.

The voice clicked off and the music started, a kind of generic free form space jam and the Rotor jerked to a start and slowly started to spin. Riders were laughing, hands flat against the wall, gripping uneasily on the smooth metal wall to keep balanced. Across from me the twins were holding hands; one of the double daters looked seasick.

The overhead bright light suddenly clicked off and above us, the dark night sky became our dim nightlight.

"Enjoy the ride!" boomed the Wizard of Oz voice out of the speaker.

The room spun faster and the music blasted. One double dater screamed.

The click-click-click of jean rivets scraping against the metal walls became a rhythmic swoosh. I heard a man's nervous laugh as the Rotor haltingly sped up, like a treadmill gaining momentum. I tried to grab Susan's hand but she had pulled her fingers into an ecstatic fist.

The Rotor spun faster and the air became a whoosh, became a thing almost visible, an almost pressure I could feel, like competing hands somehow both pushing and pulling me into the wall at the same time. The air became louder, like the roar of a waterfall. Across from me, the face of the skinny girl with braces pushed into a rubbery grin; her metallic mouth glinting randomly like Morse Code, in the cyclone of her crazy hair.

Faster and faster we spun and then we all felt a clunky shift and grinding of gears and slowly the floor began to sink away until it disappeared. Then a creak and another awkward shifting of rusty gears, a hesitation, and the Rotor tilted 45 degrees. The giant cylinder was spinning so fast I was losing track of where I was – I was in the same place but also seemingly opposite of myself.

The rings of neon suddenly switched on, circling us, dyeing us an extraterrestrial and transparent purple. I pointed my toes, dipping into an empty ocean. I was standing on air. The centrifugal force was pinning me to the spinning wall. The Rotor spun even faster, the thick halo of sound, the demented music of the midway punctured by screams and cries and shouts, all somehow terrified and exhilarated at the same time.

I swear I was lifted off the speeding wall. I hovered. My solidity was dissolving; animal, vegetable, mineral no more. I was transformed into a swirling mass of particle and energy. I was a galaxy. I was the Big Bang waiting to happen.

I was air.

FORTUNE

At the library there was a football on my calculus book, a little tightly folded origami triangle. I pried open one flap of the paper package and I folded and flipped and unfolded and flipped, then smoothed the sheet of notebook paper with my palm: "The BEST thing about this place is that if I got killed here, nobody would ever notice."

I had no idea who had left it. I looked up to see just two other people in the room. One, an old woman reading a supermarket circular very seriously, like it was an encyclopedia. Her lips mouthed "Oranges 99 cents a pound."

At the other table was a man. From where I sat, he looked vague. It was as if a police sketch artist was told to draw a man, any man. But it was his hands that I will never forget – hands that looked and acted like someone else's. He examined them in disbelief; fanning them, grabbing the air and forming empty fists.

He was surrounded by careful piles. In the center was a beat up copy of *Fortune* magazine, the April issue, with a giant calculator on the cover, and a stack of TV guides. On one side was a ROYGBIV rainbow of magic markers and on the other was a tower of graph paper, sectioned into complicated columns. He pecked and poked at the giant magazine calculator photo, using it, like a calculator, then recorded his results with the magic markers. I began to see and feel the ebb and flow to his movements.

Weeks happened. I wasn't always there, but he was; his piles of paper moved around, height growing and shrinking like some sort of strong, private graph.

I began to find things hidden in my books, tiny things: a feather, a playing card, a square of comic from the Sunday newspaper. At home I lined them up on my desk and they began to form a sort of rebus, a disjointed narrative punctuated with a rock or a bottle cap. A new language for the two of us, pieced together, more hieroglyphic than words.

Why me? I'm not sure. Maybe because I was the only person in the room. Maybe we ended up in that library to save each other. It was organic but inevitable. There was both a force field pulling us together and an invisible barrier somewhere in the middle. We used the library's code of silence as our crutch, or at least I did. Any direct communication would break the whole thing. It was the easiest excuse of the terminally shy and perpetually terrified.

Our routine was comfortable and comforting. I studied, he calculated, ten feet away. Sometimes he paused, finger mid-air, considering his computations. Once, he noiselessly unwrapped a candy bar and accordioned it into his mouth. His cheeks puffed like a trumpet players as he chewed and chewed. He saw me watching, instantly blushed, two hands rushing to hide his mouth.

The sad-faced librarian seemed resigned. "At least he's quiet," she said to me at the water fountain, as she watched me slip today's offering, a tiny plastic spider, into my pocket.

That final Thursday felt different. He was there in his usual place. The piles weren't piles anymore but a growing chaos on the table and floor. He was agitated and his hands seemed like they were fighting against him, trying to escape. Then I saw that they were covered with numbers, magic markered numbers. His wild hands and shirt were scribbled over with columns and equations. His arms looked like coloring books.

He stood up, looked at me and drew a red zero on his forehead. Then he held out the magic marker to me. I scribbled a zero on my forehead too, then took his hands to quiet them and started to cry.

They dragged him out – two policeman and the sad-faced librarian in a saggy blazer. He tried frantically to fill a dirty plastic bag with his papers, but the sad-faced woman shook her head no, saying, "We can come back for the rest tomorrow." Of course, there would be no tomorrow. She grabbed the bulging bag with one hand and him by the elbow, steering him to the door. A terrible liquid quietly dripped from the plastic bag, marking their escape trail.

I sat staring at his mess for a long time. The librarian silently filled a small metal trash can with his left behind papers and pens and candy wrappers. On top, she carefully placed the *Fortune* magazine. "I think he'd want you to take care of all this for him."

I slowly walked the ten blocks home, shifting my awkward bundle from arm to arm. The metal trash can became warm with the sun. Birds like parentheses were in the sky.

When I got home I locked my bedroom door and emptied the trash can on the floor and started to sort everything back into the familiar piles. Notepads, *TV Guides*, markers. The *Fortune* magazine calculator was destroyed; the + sign was now just a hole in the paper and all the numbers were worn off from the constant poking. And crammed inside the magazine was a cheap cassette tape. The label had been x'ed out to anonymity.

I pulled out my cassette deck and popped it in. Silence then static then BOOM. The voice in mid-sentence startled me "...I'd never ask for this back. It would be like taking back the Grand Canyon. And you'll need both hands and all of eternity to understand." The voice was twangy and distinct; it didn't match his faraway face.

I cleaned off my bureau and recreated his library setup, popping the piles into the tabletop template I remembered. For weeks afterward, I played the cassette while I flipped through the TV guides or added random digits to the thousands on the pages. His hands and phrases interrupted the litany of numbers he recited, "I'm like a leaf, too tired to unfold."

Everything shifted. I had thought of him as the radio, broadcasting for the whole world. Now I felt like a little kid, believing her favorite songs were not a record but an entire orchestra playing in a room, just for me. In a way, it was moving backward, regressing; but for me it was an odd progress. I began to understand, to trust his absence.

He was a rock, always there for me, that would not roll away.

I slept with the cassette player on the pillow next to me, switched on low, his voice whispering in the dark to me. As I drifted to sleep, his sentences became slow sounds, his words became a hypnotic hiss, a strange white noise. It was like communications with a ghost. Sometimes the cassette deck shifted in the night and in the morning it left a sleeping dent in the pillow next to me as if his head had been near mine after all.

The sad-faced librarian has been saving his note for me for weeks.

He was waiting for me at the corner. Out of the library he was different, the context had changed. He was eating an onion like an apple and when he saw me see him, he took a last bite and threw it down.

We walked down silent sidewalks, the cement threatening to disappear and then miraculously turned perpendicular, stretching another block. An awkward cloud bumped across the sky like a wad of paper thrown up and over our heads.

My question was easier to ask while we both looked straight ahead at an invisible horizon. "What did it feel like while it was happening?"

"It's complicated. I was somehow watching. It was weird and it was weirdly normal, so matter of fact."

I interrupted him. "Almost everything is weirdly normal. I remember going to New York City as a kid and watching a bum read the *New York Times*. It seemed so exotic to me – the *Times*! But then I understood that it was normal for him. What is normal depends on who you are and where you are."

"It felt normal," he said. "Unalarming, almost comforting. I just had to do those calculations. Time was of the essence. It was vital, logical even, that I add, subtract, multiply and divide all the numbers I could find in the *TV Guide* – the channels, times and dates. There was a code to break, a message, a pattern to make sense of, in all those digits.

"I pounded away at that ridiculous magazine cover calculator – it was urgent that I record the data. And at the same time, I realized it was pointless. I was furious at myself but powerless to stop. It would be like yelling at a blind man for being blind.

"I'm trying to explain it right, something that felt so otherworldly. Like when you wake up with the flu and your hair hurts? You actually feel your hair, it feels heavy and tingly, even oppressive? When 99% of the time your hair is just a dead, benign, practically weightless cloud? When you don't really acknowledge a body part's existence until something goes wrong? I became hyper aware of my hands. They felt alive and increasing out of control."

"I think I get it," I said. "But it's like you lived in a universe that was only visible to you. Like some sort of forcefield that is spinning all around you and protecting you with this weird energy."

We walked around another corner and down a street that instantly turned everything grey, different shades of grey, as if we walked through the screen of a black and white TV. City blocks of featureless apartment buildings and mysterious corner stores that sold everything and nothing. Busses were always one block ahead of us, hesitatingly tracing the curbs, intersection to intersection, burping out bursts of grey smoke.

"This is me," he said, pointing to the third grey cinder block rectangle-low, anonymous. Windows were simple squares puncturing the perimeter at irregular intervals; a few if them had metal bars, others noisy air conditioners still wrapped in tattered wintertime plastic.

He paused outside the door marked 4F. "I don't have people over. Ever. I don't even like to be here and I live here."

"But why stay?" I asked.

"I don't suppose I'm unhappier here than I should be anywhere else," he answered, as he struggled with the key and pushed the door with a shoulder. He walked into the grayness and groped the air, finally catching the pull cord for the ceiling bulb. CLICK. Nothing happened.

"Hold on." He tapped his foot searchingly next to the apartment door until we both heard a metallic thud and then a rolling sound. "My flashlight." Another click and a small tube of light bisected the room.

Boxes. Hundreds of boxes, stacked along the walls, floor to ceiling. It was like being inside a bunker made of cardboard boxes. Even the windows were covered. Small piles of newspapers were configured into furniture – chairs, couch, a tiny table. In the center of the room was a big orange tent.

"This is it." He pointed at the tent. "When it's all lit up inside, it's like sleeping in a volcano."

He unzipped the giant nickel zipper of the half moon door and we stooped inside the orange dome. The walls undulated almost like breaths as we shifted inside, inflating and deflating with our movements. The floor, a strange and spongy topography of dirty laundry had a long valley down the center. I slid into the warm groove and propped my arm up on the mountain range of socks and shirts and scratchy sweaters; it felt like a shoulder, and a little lower, a hip.

He watched as I found a handhold and then suddenly he bulldozed the dark pile and filled in the C-shaped valley beside me, and pulled my hand around his waist. The glow of the flashlight lit up the orange tent all around us and it was warm inside and alive. It really was like being inside a volcano. And when he finally started to talk, to explain all the rest of his lifetime, it was in a very clear voice.

ACME

The Jehovah's Witnesses were driving me crazy with their too-polite knocks and damnation pamphlets. Maybe they earned extra credit for early morning salvation attempts? I was always too sleepy to answer and peeked thru the peephole at their church lady hats and cheap briefcases as they walked to the curb. Martha at the hardware store was one. She had hair she could sit on and I saw her eating a bowl of cereal on the bus. She once showed me a little laminated card in her wallet – NUNCA SANGRA – blood transfusions were not allowed even if you were dying in the street.

Maybe the Jehovah's did the math and figured the odds were on their side; after dozens of mornings of relentless knocking, I answered the door on Saturday. With dripping hair and wrapped in a towel, I swung the door open dramatically.

"Good morning," said the lone guy who was most definitely not a Jehovah's Witness.

"Oh," I answered, my hand reassuring the knotted terrycloth around my chest.

"This actually happens all the time," the young man said. His hair was the color of a manila envelope and obviously cut while blindfolded. His eyes were the most boring eyes in the world – just dots really – but his smile was so ridiculous, so dazzling – like a movie star, like a billboard for toothpaste.

"I was praying the towel would finally scare off the Witnesses," I blurted out.

"I'm not scared, but I'm not one of them." He held up clipboard; a pencil on a string dangled from it. "I ask questions."

"Door to door?" I asked.

"Door to door," he nodded.

He was wearing a light blue workshirt with an embroidered ACME patch over the pocket. It seemed vaguely professional.

"I will answer your questions," I told him. "Come with me to the Laundromat and ask me questions from your clipboard."

He followed me into the kitchen. The small TV on the counter was turned to the Spanish soap opera. Louisa shouted at Ricardo – "*Donde esta mi madre*?" – I pushed some magazines off the second chair and Acme sat down. "I watch this to keep my Spanish from getting rusty. The main thing to remember is that '*Estoy embarazada*' does not mean what it sounds like. It means 'I'm pregnant.' I found out the hard way."

Acme laughed.

I spooned two tablespoons of instant coffee into two mugs and poured boiling water from a small saucepan. The brown grains swirled to the surface until I propellored the spoon and they dissolved with the heat. I handed Acme his coffee and grabbed an elementary-school-lunch-sized milk carton from the almost empty refrigerator. "Have you seen me?" was written on three sides, next to a postage stamp of a photo of a girl with a crooked smile and startled eyes.

I plopped down in the other kitchen chair and we sipped our coffee. "You are still in your Jehovah"s Witness towel," Acme pointed out.

"I know. I do laundry every Saturday. Every piece I own except this towel. We can wheel over to the Laundromat after coffee."

"Not that I mind," said Acme. "I just wondered." He noisily slurped his coffee. "This is probably the worst coffee I've ever had."

I laughed. "The coffee at the Laundromat is even

worse. Somehow you can even taste the styrofoam cup."

We sat quietly. Outdoor sounds squeezed in through the half-opened window – a man coughing, an outburst of barking, a plane jetting overhead and then fading away.

I tucked my feet under my chair and slid them back out on top of white canvas tennis shoes, the backs bent in, flattened. Using my pointer finger as a shoe horn, I wedged on the still doubled knotted sneakers.

"Ready for our adventure?" I asked, as I buttoned up my raincoat over the Jehovahs Witness towel.

The wire grocery cart was waiting next to the front door; the lumpy cloth laundry bags oozed through the slats like mashed potatoes.

Acme grabbed his clipboard and we wheeled the cart down the sidewalk towards the Laundromat. The handfuls of laundry quarters in my coat pockets rattled as I tripped over every bump in the cement I did not see.

"Ok, first question – why are you just wearing a towel and washing all your clothes at once?"

I sighed. "The Four F's, I guess. Fire, flood, famine, father."

Acme looked confused. "Five F's – one is for follow up. Please."

I rolled my eyes. "My dad was a fireman so he drilled it into me to always be prepared."

"Prepared for what?"

"Prepared for anything. To save time, to escape as quickly as possible. At night I got my breakfast 90% ready – cereal poured into the bowl, two pieces of bread poised in the toaster, the pre-buttered knife diagonal on the plate. All I had to do in the morning was push the toaster button.

"He would do time trials to see how long it would take me to get out of the house. I never knew when they would happen. Sometimes the smoke alarm would go off after midnight. I once caught him standing on a chair in the hallway, exhaling an entire pack of cigarettes in front of the smoke detector.

"Every rung of the escape ladder shook as I climbed down in the dark. The blackness was only broken by my father directing his powerful flashlight at me, like one of those helicopters looking for fugitives from the sky.

"A few times he blasted the referee in a can – that metal tube with a horn attached. He stood in the driveway and squeezed it mercilessly. Of course the neighbors hated him. And he used a stopwatch. I wore my nightgown over my school clothes. It helped me feel at least outwardly normal. It also cut seconds off my escape time.

"No matter how often the drills happened – sometimes it was months between them and other times they were back to back – there was a constant fear of sleep. Each drill was a crazy adrenaline rush. I needed to run off the extra energy surge and I'd stand in the dark living room and jog in place until I was finally exhausted."

"Jesus," Acme said, shaking his head.

"My father wrote down my times in a pocket notebook he kept with him at all times. Rows of numbers, colored pencil charts and graphs. It wasn't until he disappeared, the day he emptied his pockets onto the kitchen counter and calmly walked out the door, that I began to understand what he had done. How he had negated every single day for a future of emergency and disaster that never happened. I realized how much time was lost, wasted.

"He unplugged every lamp, every appliance, but the refrigerator, at night. He blamed faulty electrical work for most household fires. I learned to see in the dark, to feel my way around the house, to trace the outline of furniture, doorways, with my hands; count out the necessary steps to the bathroom. It was like living in a Braille coloring book. I slept with the curtains open to get even a sliver of street light into my room."

"Did you ever sleep?" Acme asked.

"I learned to sleep at weird times in weird places. Snoring in the shower, catnaps in the cafeteria. Even now, beds seem dangerous. I still make my bed with all the sheets at once, one on top of the other. That first night, it's like I've built a force field around me. And every morning, I peel off a layer, like an onion, and my protection shrinks by that precious millimeter."

We paused at the intersection. Acme turned towards me, the sun blazing and outrageous behind him. Suddenly his hair was orange, like it was on fire and his skin was transparent. Red and blue veins that had been invisible suddenly made a nonsensical roadmap of his forehead, his neck. It was as if he had been turned inside out.

He was talking to me, but I was tuned out, distracted by the gentle pulsating in his temple. His talk no longer words but just sounds, like the teacher in Charlie Brown. Then I noticed the blood trickle, ever so slowly, from his nose, outline his upper lip and then drip down his chin and onto his blue shirt. The blood blossomed into a spidery red flower. My eyes refocused, and startled, I asked, "Are you ok?"

Acme reflexively rubbed his face, smearing the blood with his fingertips, then looked at his hand. "I'm sorry. It happens."

I poked around in my dirty laundry and handed him a gym sock. "Thanks. People around here are used to it. Sometimes they even seem kind of disappointed if I don't bleed." Wearing my sock like a puppet, Acme tilted his head back and pinched his nostrils. The blood soaked his fingertips and striped the white cotton sock on his arm.

Acme and I stopped on the sidewalk, his head tilted back, looking at the sky, hoping for gravity to stop the blood. A bowlegged woman in a terrible housecoat was waiting outside the Laundromat, her tiny dog impatient and tangled around her concave ankles. At her feet, a thank-you-for-shopping-here plastic bag was dropped, a box of popsicles melting into a rainbow puddle. A few noisy bees and a line of ants were drinking in the sweet decay. The dog was licking its feet.

"We're here," I laughed and pushed open the door. I wheeled my overloaded cart in like a drunk driver.

"Good morning, young lady," called out Miss Helen, the attendant.

She was the oldest woman in the world, a skeleton really, ruling in her secondhand upholstered armchair, aluminum TV tray at her side. Miss Helen wore plaid polyester pants and a faded sweatshirt, a fistful of tissues tucked underneath one wristband. Nobody had ever seen her out of that chair.

Acme looked at Miss Helen and whispered, "Is it really her job to sit there all day?"

"She runs a tight ship. Her dead husband opened this place a million years ago."

I walked over to Miss Helen. "I'm renting one of your *National Enquirers* until my laundry is done," I said, and tossed a quarter into the mayonnaise jar on her tray. She nodded. I waved the yellowed tabloid in the air: Dolly Parton Shocker! "This looks good!"

The Laundromat was a big square bisected by a long countertop on skinny legs. On one wall were the portholes of the industrial washers and on the other leg of the L, were the dryers. A row of molded plastic chairs, segmented like a caterpillar, ran along the steamy windows.

Acme, still pinching his bloody nose, looked around fascinated. He watched the woman leaning against a washer, holding a paper cup, ringed with old coffee like an ancient tree. Her movements were slow and stiff, a rusted robot, as she brought the cup to her lips. "It's like a meeting of Sleepwalkers Anonymous in here."

"It is another world," I agreed. "Planet Fluff and Fold."

I dumped my laundry onto the big table and sorted it into piles to wash. Acme talked, the gym sock muffling his voice, like a kid trying to do impressions. The blood on his shirt was growing, climbing its way across his chest.

"I think my nosebleed finally stopped but my shirt looks like a crime scene." Acme slowly unbuttoned his shirt with wet fingers, dotting the fabric with bloody halfmoons.

"Tshirt too," I commanded.

He sat there, shirtless in the plastic chair, looking at his reflection in the round glass of the dryer door and wiping his nose with the sock. His skin was so pale, he glowed.

"No shirt, no shoes, no service," I reminded him, pointing to the cardboard sign scotch taped to the wall. "Miss Helen is very strict about topless customers. That's why I wear my trenchcoat." I handed him a bedsheet. He knotted it around his neck like a cape.

He washed the blood off his face in the water fountain, his features distorted like a funhouse mirror in the molded metal. Then he held his shirt above the spout and the arc of water blasted clean the center of the bloody stain. The shirt turned brown, then pale, then a rusty shadow. He tossed the wet shirts into the drum of the washer and they thwacked solidly, like a fish slapped onto a dock. The quarters activated the machine and it gradually came to life – the steady bursts of water, the sporadic release of detergent, the increasingly rhythmic agitator.

Acme in his cape, me in my towel – we quietly watched the portal of the washing machine as if it was the most fascinating movie in the world. It was soothing and hypnotic.

"I told you about the midnight ladders and why I am sitting here, now, with you, in a Laundromat. So how did you start going door-to-door with your clipboard asking strangers questions?"

"See that guy over there?" Acme asked. "The guy in the grey space suit?" He tilted his head toward the fat man folding dozens of pairs of underwear into tidy origami packets. He was wearing a puffy plastic jumpsuit, with thick elastic cuffs at the wrists and ankles. It was like elephant skin.

"That's George. The first time I saw him I was 8 years old and assumed he was an astronaut. He was in his front yard, raking leaves in his inflatable suit."

George was whistling. I noticed the rubber gasket with a big knob, attached at the belly button, on his crinkly jumpsuit. I suddenly realized it was an inflatable sauna suit from the back of *Parade Magazine*, the kind that plug into the vacuum cleaner hose for extra reduction powers.

"I always wondered who actually bought those diet suits," I said to Acme. "The FDA outlawed those things when people got dehydrated and passed out in the middle of Kmart."

Acme said, "George never seems to get any smaller but he always seems hopeful, even when his suit is deflated. He stopped wearing real clothes decades ago. He even wears it grocery shopping. When I saw him pushing that cart filled with paper towels and Tang, I assumed he was an off-duty astronaut. That's the beauty of a uniform, even a half-baked one – your identity is never questioned."

I watched George methodically pairing up his clean

tube socks, his plastic suit rustling loudly like candy wrappers in a movie theatre.

"I'd see George," Acme continued, "and shyly ask him questions about outer space because I was obsessed with the moon. George never actually said he was in NASA, never once agreed with my crazy science fiction-fueled theories. But he never said no either, never denied my assumptions. I'd ask him stuff like 'What's it like up there?' and he'd answer 'Dark. And, ummm…cold?'"

"Did the other kids think he was an astronaut too?"

"I was never sure," Acme answered. "I felt like it was our special connection, that I was the only one smart enough to guess his top secret secret. After all, it's more exciting to talk about peeing in zero-gravity than sitting in a broken Barcalounger and watching *Wheel of Fortune* all day. It was a secret that made us both happier.

"A few years later I found a balled up polyester Burger King uniform in a bus stop. It smelled like a million french fries. I'm not sure why, but I pulled it over my Tshirt and wore it home. Strangers asked me questions about my job, like if I could drink unlimited milkshakes. Just by putting on a different shirt, I became a different person. It seemed so easy, maybe too easy, to not be me. Suddenly I understood George, and how it was easier to just go along with things.

"I wondered who else I could become. I looked for mechanics shirts at the thrift shop. I'd find supermarket cashier smocks abandoned on sidewalks in a minimum wage rage. I had a drawerful of termite exterminator sweatshirts and a faded lifeguard tank top. I'd put on a uniform and go to a part of the city I didn't know and plop myself down in a coffee shop all day. People would ask me questions, treat me like an expert. It felt good to be an authority on something. I had been fired from every real job I had ever had. I was a pizza delivery guy with no sense of direction. I somehow left open all the ferret cages at the pet shop and couldn't mow a straight line at the golf course."

I laughed and turned to look at Acme. He was staring straight ahead at the washing machine as he spoke. He sighed and adjusted the bedsheet knotted around his neck. I looked at the washer. Framed in the shiny glass door, the wet white laundry was sloppy and spinning, suds dotted the water. A lonely red sock swirled among the towels and Tshirts, spiraling like a giant peppermint candy, first in one direction and then in reverse. The air was humid from the endless cycles of clothes dryers drying. Miss Helen dramatically fanned herself with a rolled up *Weekly World News*.

"But what made you stop answering questions and

start asking them from door to door?"

Acme shifted in the plastic chair. "I was wearing a starched lab coat and a teenager offered me a cruller if I gave her a second opinion on her upcoming gall bladder surgery. I realized *Readers Digest* medical knowledge was a dangerous thing. So I told her I was a veterinarian. She was disappointed."

A small boy in Batman pajamas set up a tiny bowling alley on the floor next to the industrial washers. We watched as he rolled a dirty tennis ball into a triangle of miniature boxes of Tide detergent from the vending machine. Some were full and some were torn open, and with each collision a cloud of grit and blinding dust exploded into the air like spores.

Sometimes when the ball missed the kid kicked the boxes over with his foot and satisfied, smiled.

Acme looked at me. "Those miniature detergents are just like the fun-size boxes of cereal I used to beg my father to buy for me. I loved to cut along the dotted lines and fold back the cardboard wings. It was like a camping trip in your hand."

George sat across from us and rested a can of orange soda on the shelf of his stomach. The Laundromat got hotter with each load of clothes thrown into a dryer. His face was flushed and sweaty. George wiped his forehead with a bandanna then retucked it into the cuff of his suit. With each fidget his plastic space suit noisily suctioned and unsuctioned onto the molded plastic chair, breathing, moving, almost as if it was alive. I looked at George's wrinkled wrists, imprinted with years of elastic, and I thought about all those years spent mummified in plastic, his body cut off from air, from the world, so much that it was gradually losing its elasticity, its color, that it was starting to resemble the plastic suit he wore like a suit of armor.

Acme pointed to Washer 17. "It's winding down," he said, as it did a lethargic last spin. He pulled out an armful of wet laundry and looked at it helplessly. "I need a dryer."

I found one and he dumped it all in. The front of his bedsheet cape was heavy and grey with a circle of damp; the back hung and billowed. I pulled out quarters from the pocket of my trenchcoat and slid them into the slot. The wet laundry thumped clumsily as it slowly began to spin, picking up momentum. George slurped is soda. Acme leaned over and said quietly, "I'm scared George will become one of those shut ins who refuse to leave their vinyl recliners for years and eat cases of potato chips and their skin eventually fuses into the cushions. Somehow they lose themselves..."

I finished his sentence, "...and become a chair with a face."

“Exactly,” said Acme. “It’s scary. George went from an astronaut to a Lazy Boy recliner all because of that stupid jumpsuit. It seemed like too much baggage. The gall bladder question – the responsibility – shook me up and I threw it all out, every uniform I had. But the Acme shirt seemed different. It was universal but somehow vague. I carried a clipboard and everything shifted. Strangers stopped asking me to diagnose the weird clanking in their dishwashers. I asked the questions.

“The first questions are always easy, to build up their confidence, like those $100 categories on Jeopardy. Then things snowball from specifics like ‘Left handed or right handed?’ to ‘Would you ever parachute into a volcano?’ to a zinger like ‘Tell me about the time you were most disappointed by your parents.’”

The dryers hummed and the washers thwacked all around us. The air felt thick with dampness and heat. The whole place had that yeasty smell of lint. Miss Helen shimmied in her chair and used both hands to lift her limp left leg over her right knee, an oddly ladylike gesture. Her left foot dangled and shook.

“I ran out of my own questions after the first week. I underestimated how excited people were to talk about themselves. No one was surprised, no one refused to answer. I started an endless master list of questions. I stole from everywhere – Cosmo magazine, crackpot pop psychology books, supermarket scandal sheets. Even Bazooka Joe comics. Somehow the randomness made it all seem oddly legitimate. I took some notes, but mostly the interviews became meandering monologues. I nodded a lot.

People finished, unburdened and exhausted. They even looked lighter and brighter, more buoyant. Some glowed."

I looked at Acme. "It sounds like going to confession with scientist. And without the phone booth."

"It is. And I even have the cape," he said, flapping the bedsheet around his shoulders.

"Don't underestimate the power of a cape or a trenchcoat."

We watched the dryers spin. As the minutes passed, the wet clothes tumbled and incrementally fluffed up behind the glass doors, like whipped cream.

"Ask me a question," I said, slightly dizzy from watching the dryers

"Here's a good one. What's your favorite vehicle?"

"It's a tie. A golf cart and a cement mixer."

"Why am I not surprised," Acme said.

"I'm pretty predictable. So what's yours?"

"An elevator."

"That does not count."

"It counts. It moves."

"Maybe I should borrow your demented dictionary," I said.

The dryer spun, then paused, then noisily shifted gears for a final reverse spin. We watched the digital red numbers count down. Two minutes, then one. Click! The hot laundry crackled with electricity. I pulled at a knot of stuck socks, stretching them like saltwater taffy. Sparks fireflied into the air. Acme flapped his knotted bedsheet like a dimestore Dracula.

The windows of the Laundromat were dreamy and foggy. At eye level, circles and slashes were rubbed out by fingers to see the world outside. I took off my trench-coat. Side by side, we sorted the laundry. Faint ghosts of warmth pulsated from the piles of socks and shirts and skirts. I dug out Acme's shirt, grabbed it by the shoulders and shook it out. It was hot – alive again – like skin, as I put it on.

About the Author

Lauren Leja is a writer, photographer, snapshot collector and rescuer of the forgotten. She has a website, invisiblecommute.com, in which she documents her wanderings with a daily photo. Lauren's first book, *Air and other stories*, was published by Nixes Mate in 2017.

42° 19′ 47.9″ N 70° 56′ 43.9″ W

Nixes Mate is a navigational hazard in Boston Harbor used during the colonial period to gibbet and hang pirates and mutineers.

Nixes Mate Books features small-batch artisanal literature, created by writers who use all 26 letters of the alphabet and then some, honing their craft the time-honored way: one line at a time.

nixesmate.pub/books

www.ingramcontent.com/pod-product-compliance
Lightning Source LLC
Chambersburg PA
CBHW070507170726
48291CB00008B/2686